I Love You More

EMIL SHER

illustrations by
BARBARA REID

North Winds Press
An Imprint of Scholastic Canada Ltd.

I love you more

than flowers love noses.

I love you more
than erasers
love mistakes.

I love you more than icing loves cakes.

I love you more than blackboards love chalk.

I love you more

than cones love ice cream.

I love you more
than syrup loves pancakes.

I love you more
than laces love shoes.

I love you more
than umbrellas love rain.

I love you more
than string loves kites.

I love you more
than stars love wishes.

I love you more
than green loves spring.

I love you more

than hats love heads.

I love you more
than pianos love hands.

I love you more than trees love nests.

Now It's Your Turn

As young children, my two daughters spent a slice of their summers at sleepover camp. At the end of our letters to them, my wife drew a beautiful, leap-off-the-page red heart. I searched for a way to express my bottomless love through words. *I love you more than runways love planes. More than easels love paintings. More than answers love question marks.* Soon my daughters ended their letters in the same way. *I love you more than sponges love spills. More than patches love holes. More than graters love cheese.*

This kind of word game always comes in pairs, and in a certain order: the second part of the pair makes the first part feel happy because it feels needed. *I love you more than mistakes love erasers* isn't wrong, but it isn't quite right. A mistake doesn't have to be erased. It can be circled, crossed out, underlined. But when an eraser sees a mistake, it jumps for joy (if erasers could jump). Whenever you think of a pairing, start with the half that feels valued by the other half (like cones to ice cream).

My daughters have long since grown up, but we continue to play this word game. Now you can play it wherever you go, wherever you are. It's suitable for all ages. All you need is a few words, and a lot of love.

— *Emil Sher*

For Julian and Ilona, and their armfuls of
love for a grateful kid brother.
— E.S.

For my D.O.L.D.
— B.R.

The illustrations for this book were made with modelling clay that is
shaped and pressed onto illustration board.

Photography by Ian Crysler

Library and Archives Canada Cataloguing in Publication
Title: I love you more / Emil Sher ; illustrated by Barbara Reid.
Names: Sher, Emil, 1959- author. | Reid, Barbara, 1957- illustrator.
Description: Published simultaneously in softcover by Scholastic Canada Ltd.
Identifiers: Canadiana 20210229861 | ISBN 9781443175807 (hardcover)
Classification: LCC PS8587.H38535 I22 2022 | DDC jC813/.54—dc23

www.scholastic.ca

6 5 4 3 2 1   Printed in China 62   22 23 24 25 26 27

FSC
MIX
Paper from
responsible sources
FSC® C020056
www.fsc.org